Border Bob's

James Ross

Special thanks to Jas for putting up with me living in my head for much of the time, to Laura for being an enthusiastic critical reader, to Chiara for her fantastic artwork, and an extra special thankyou to my own Border Terrier, Angus, the inspiration and original audience for these stories

Artwork by Chiara Mendicino

"Dogs and Angels are not very far apart."

Charles Bukowski

Introduction:

Border Bob is a little brown dog who lives in a cosy kennel at the side of the Big House – real name Craigmorley House - in the border region between England and Scotland. Every morning, Bob likes to wander the grounds of the Big House, searching for signs of Mr. Fox, or snaffling food from the kitchen, and he enjoys lying at his kennel door watching the world go by.

Bob knows that his Main Job is to protect the people in the Big House and especially to look after The Girl. He often visits Stan the Stable-boy, who gives him treats and pets him a lot. Some days, when Lord Craigmorley takes his favourite horse Mercy for a ride, Bob will dash along beside them across field and brook, through gates and

beneath hedges, though, after an hour or two, Bob

sometimes needs a rest and hitches a ride home inside the

Big Man's coat.

Craigmorley: The 'Big House'.

In the winter, Bob is kept very cosy because his kennel has

a large blanket that was given to him by The Girl, on which

he can snuggle up and stay warm. Sometimes, he sneaks

into the study where the Big Man spends his evenings, and squashes in between the Big Man's Irish Wolfhounds, Brian and Boru. They don't mind because they know Bob is feisty, friendly, and he doesn't take up too much space.

This little book is about a particular Christmas that took place a long time ago, when Bob was a little over two years old, and when some magical events occurred.

November

Wee Jock the postman considered himself a very fortunate man. He'd grown up in a tiny house in the village of Mindrum, one of eleven children, he nearly always had food to eat, and with six older siblings (as well as four younger ones), there was usually a pair of shoes to fit, and his clothes, if well-worn, were always clean and mended. When he was fifteen years-old, Wee Jock went away to the war. He looked splendid in his uniform, he marched proudly, and he ate three good meals a day. Again, he was very lucky, gaining hardly a scratch, apart from that pesky shrapnel in his arm, and a touch of the gas on his chest. When Jock returned home he was very lucky to get a job as a postman, and he only had to ride twenty-five or thirty miles a day on his old iron bike, and if the hills between delivery stops never got less steep, the freewheels down the other side never got less fun. Even the dogs on his delivery route loved Wee Jock because he kept a small bag of boiled sweets in his pocket and gave one to each dog, so that instead of barking and chasing him, the dogs welcomed him, chewing happily on their granny sookers and toffee drops. Jock's favourite dog was a little Border Terrier called Bob, who lived at Craigmorley House.

However, early one morning, for the first time in his life, Wee Jock thought that perhaps, his luck had run out.

He had been cycling along the Tweedmouth Road with a bag full of mail to deliver when snow began to fall. It was unexpected so early in the year, but, never mind, he thought, I have my thick woollen coat to keep me warm, and my peaked cap to keep the snow off my head. He delivered mail to all the homes along the border - Mr

Douglas the farmer, old Mrs. Darling and her Bulldog

Edward, and many more homes too - but the snow kept on

falling and the road became white and slippy.

Finally, disaster struck!

Letters and packages were strewn everywhere!

The front wheel of his bike hit a patch of ice and he

skidded and crashed into a ditch. Letters and packages

were strewn everywhere! When he tried to get up he

realised he had injured his leg and could not stand. And

still, the snow kept falling. Perhaps my luck has finally run out he thought to himself, as he sat shivering in the ditch.

Snow began to cover his shoulders and his black peaked

cap quickly turned white.

Meanwhile, in his cosy kennel at the side of the Big House,

a little brown dog lay watching the road as the snow fell.

Border Bob, the doggie in question, knew that every

morning, the little man on his strange machine came down

the path specially to give him a sweet. Bob liked sweets. He

liked the little man. Bob knew that the man visited

specially to see him, to give him a treat and to tell him he

was a good boy. So, he waited. And the snow continued to

fall.

Bob didn't know what a clock was, but he knew that the

little man who brought him treats was late. Curious, he

stood and stretched, then trotted out into the snow to

look for the man. And his treats.

Bob trotted along the drive, then followed his nose in the direction from which the man usually came. After a while Bob was covered in snow, but his thick double-coat provided lots of warmth and so Bob happily trotted along to see why the little man had not brought him a treat.

After a while he heard a noise coming from the side of the road. Curious, he looked into the ditch and saw a strange white shape, in the middle of which he spotted the face of the little man!

'Come here, Bob!' Wee Jock shouted. 'Good boy! Come here and see your postie. There's a good boy!'

Bob knew he was a good boy and he padded with his little paws over to where the man lay in the snow. He sniffed the man, and then sniffed at his pocket.

'You'd like a boiled sweetie, eh Bob?' the man said, putting a hand into his pocket and taking out two sweets. Two! Bob took them and crunched them happily, then licked the little man's hands to say thank you.

The little man reached into his postbag, and took out a roll of twine and a label, and with a pencil that was in his coat pocket he scribbled message on the back of the label. He fastened the label round Bob's neck as carefully as he could, his fingers were shaking with the cold. Bob didn't mind if he had to wear a collar - it usually meant he was going somewhere special, but all the little man said was 'Away home, Bob! Away home!' Bob sniffed the man's pocket again. 'Here you are,' the man said, giving Bob another sweetie. 'Now away home!'

Bob turned and trotted home.

The snow was deep and Bob sometimes had to jump so that his feet could clear the snow. A lesser dog might have got tired but not Bob, for Bob was a Border Terrier and he was born for the inclement and changeable weather of the borders, his paws had extra fur on them to keep them warm, and long claws to dig into the snow and get a grip. Still, he was a little tired when he got back to the Big House so he thought he might snaffle some food from the kitchen, or at least get warm and cosy. He nosed quietly through the kitchen door and stepped into the bright warmth and the lovely smells, and he shook his fur to get rid of the snow that was now melting on his fur.

'Get out, Bob!' Mrs. Hands the cook shouted when she saw him. 'Get outside ye wee cur!' Mrs. Hands did not like small brown dogs shaking their wet fur in her kitchen, so Bob turned to go, but just then, Hooks the Butler entered the kitchen. In the winter it was well known that the kitchen was the warmest room in the Big House, and Hooks found lots of reasons to pop in. 'What's going on?' he asked Mrs.

Hands.

'That little beastie is shaking his wet fur all over my

kitchen floor.'

'I'll see to him,' Hooks said.

Hooks was almost as tall as the Big Man, and when he

reached down to pick up Bob, he felt very strong, and Bob

didn't mind if he carried him outside, but Hooks he noticed

something. 'What's this?' He put Bob down onto the floor

and took the twine and label from Bob's neck and read it

carefully, saying to himself, 'Oh, this won't do!' he said as

he flung open the back-kitchen door and strode outside

into the snow with Bob trotting behind. 'Stan!' he shouted,

and Stan the stable-boy came out of the stable, curry

comb in his hand. 'Harness Mercy to the old sleigh, quick as

you can. Wee Jock the postman is lying injured out on the

Tweedmouth road.' He looked up at the falling snow. 'And we haven't got a moment to spare.'

In minutes, Stan had Mercy, the powerful young mare, harnessed to the old sleigh, ready in the yard. Hooks, now wrapped in an overcoat, took the driver's seat, with Stan beside him, and Bob sitting in Stan's lap, warm and cosy, only his nose and little round eyes peeping out from Stan's winter coat. Hooks shouted at Mercy, the whipped cracked in the air (not *at* Mercy, who needed no goading to trot or gallop) and horse, sleigh, men and dog moved away quickly into the snow, down the drive, then turning onto the Tweedmouth Road.

*

'Well, your leg will heal in due time,' Doctor Charlie said, his fingertips carefully checking out Wee Jock's injured leg.

'But I'm not sure that you be able to pedal that heavy old bike up the hills.'

Wee Jock's face fell.

'You should count your blessings that the wee doggie found you, Jock,' the doctor said, kindly. 'Another half hour and you'd have perished out there in the snow.

'Aye. I'm a lucky man,' Wee Jock said. He was very grateful to have been rescued, but he didn't feel too lucky. If he couldn't pedal his bike, he would lose his job as a postie.

The doctor studied Jock's crestfallen expression and knew his mind. 'You like your job, Jock?'

'I do. The fresh air. The early mornings. All the people tae say hello when I pass.'

'You even like the dogs.'

'They're ay friends to me. Especially little Bob from the Big House. He's ma wee rescuer.'

'Yes, Border Terriers are tough, helpful little dogs. But with your injury, I can see you're worried you might lose your job.'

'How can I deliver the mail wi' a gammy leg?' Jock said, his voice quavering.

The doctor looked thoughtful. 'Leave it with me, Jock McDougal,' he said firmly. 'I'll speak to the postmaster.'

And so it was that a month later, as Bob lay in his kennel sniffing the morning air, he heard a strange noise. Over the brow of the hill and down the drive came a little machine. It had four wheels and a roof, and it was bright red. They say dogs can't see the colour red very well, but Bob noticed the bright red van nevertheless. He watched as it parked in front of the house and he recognised the small man who got out of the front, a handful of letters in his hand, and limped across to the back-kitchen door. He knocked just as Bob trotted up and made a little noise to catch his attention. The kitchen door opened and Wee Jock the postman said 'Hello!' to Grace, the kitchen maid, handed her the mail and then turned to Bob.

'You're ma wee champion,' he said, ruffling Bob's fur. 'You saved ma life in the blizzard, and then the postmaster has gi'en me a brand new wagon to deliver the mail.' He reached into his pocket and took out a boiled sweet, gave it to Bob, who snapped it up and chewed happily. 'You've made me a very lucky man.'

"Wee Champion." Bob did not know these words, but he knew they meant he had been a good boy. He chewed on the boiled sweet, which tasted very nice.

He was very proud.

December

One morning in early December, Bob woke in his cosy kennel, stepped outside and stretched comfortably. The snow of the previous month had long melted, but the trees were bare and the air was very cold and it felt to Bob, though he did not know quite how he knew, that the snow would soon return.

Bob did his rounds to check for signs of Mr. Fox, he sniffed the hen coop and made his mark on various trees and posts, and after he'd been down to the riverside to smell the frosty air and lap the freezing water, he decided that today would be a perfect day for snaffling treats from the kitchen and lying in his kennel watching the world go by. However, when the people in the Big House began to wake, and the eastern sky began to lighten, Bob realised that there was a hubbub in the air. Everyone seemed to be full of energy, the smells from the oven in the kitchen were even nicer than normal, and Stan didn't have time to pet Bob for more than a minute or two before he set to cleaning the horses. Bob watched from his favourite spot in the stables as Stan cleaned and brushed the Big Man's horses, swept out the stables, and made everything spick and span. He wondered what on earth was going on?

After a while, Bob went to the kitchen door and sniffed the lovely smells as Mrs. Hands cooked fresh pies. He was surprised when Mrs. Hands came to the door and laid a bowl on the step with slices of cooked pastry, with not so much as a harsh word, but not so surprised that he didn't eat them up in seconds.

Something was up!

Though Bob didn't know it, The Girl, Bob's favourite person in all the world, was coming home from school for Christmas, and everyone wanted to make the house perfect for her return.

Bob watched Stan the stable boy start up the smelly machine that carried people about when they weren't walking or riding horses. Stan looked at Bob and clicked his tongue, so Bob trotted over. 'I'm going to Berwick Station to collect Miss Celia, Bob. Would you like to come with me?' Bob barked with joy at hearing The Girl's name, and suddenly he understood what all the fuss was about. He began to run in circles and bark happily, and Stan laughed, saying, 'Give me a moment Bob, then we'll be off. Ten minutes later, Stan was climbing into the motorcar, and waited until Bob leapt over his legs and sat in the passenger seat before closing the door. 'The train arrives at one, so we'll be there with time to spare, and we'll be

home by three,' Stan told Bob. This was important because,

by three o clock on a December afternoon, the sun in the

borders was already beginning to set, the air would turn

colder, the roads would become icy, and Stan didn't want to

be driving home in the dark on slippery roads.

They set off along the drive, turning right on the

Tweedmouth Road towards Berwick. Bob poked his head

out of the window, but the air was so cold and sharp that

after a while he sat down on the chair, and curled up.

Happy to be with Stan, and even happier to be seeing The

Girl. After two or three miles, they passed Old Mr.

Douglas' farm, then a few miles beyond that, the tiny

hamlet where Grace the kitchen maid lived with her nine

brothers and sisters and her mother and father in a tiny

cottage with a tiny kitchen in which Grace's mother

somehow managed to cook meals for her always-growing family. Finally, after an hour's journey, the little car containing Stan and Bob pulled up outside of Berwick railway station. However, just as they got to the platform they heard the station manager announce that the London train was delayed. 'I'm off to get a cup of tea,' Stan said, 'You stay there and keep watch.' Stan went into the tiny tearoom while Bob sat outside watching the people walk back and forwards. Some of the people gave him a nice pet, and one old lady gave him a toffee!

Eventually a huge smelly machine came chugging along the tracks. Bob heard it before he saw it and began to bark, just as Stan returned. The huge machine belched steam and smoke as it slowed down and stopped with a giant *hisssss*!! Doors opened and closed with a bang, people got on and got off, and then The Girl appeared. She was wearing her best traveling school uniform and looked very

smart. 'Bobbeeeeee!!!' she cried and ran up to him and gave

him lots of pets and hugs and Bob was very proud to be

greeting her at the station, even if the machine that

delivered her was loud and smelly.

A huge smelly machine came chugging along the tracks.

Stan carried her luggage back to the car and The Girl got

in the back with Bob and stroked him and hugged him as

they began driving home. After a short while it began to snow. The countryside looked beautiful in the snow but the car made slow progress as it fell heavier and thicker. In the back seat, The Girl cuddled Bob so they both kept warm and she told Bob all about school, and what she had been doing.

Suddenly, just few miles from home, the car stopped. A thick bank of snow had blocked the entire road. Stan got out and used a shovel to try and dig out the snow but it was too deep. He returned to the car, 'You and Bob stay there, Miss. I'll go to Old Douglas' farm and get some help.' Fifteen minutes later he returned with a flask of tea, a warm blanket and some cake from Mrs. Douglas. He had also brought Old Helen, one of Farmer Douglas' cart horses. Bob barked to see Helen. She was tall and powerful and Bob was impressed. 'It's too deep to tow the car,' Stan

told The Girl, so here's what we will do...'

Bob barked to see Helen. She was tall and powerful

and Bob was impressed.

And so it was that five minutes later, that Bob and The

Girl sat on Helen's broad back wrapped in a tartan blanket,

with Stan at the front holding the reins. 'Ready?' he asked,

and The Girl said yes, and Bob barked. Stan clicked his

tongue and Old Helen began walking through the deep snow carrying all three passengers back to the Big House. As they rode, The Girl secretly fed Bob pieces of Mrs. Douglas' cake.

When they arrived at the Big House, Stan slipped off Old Helen's back, and took Bob from The Girl, then he helped her down too. The Girl ran excitedly towards the door, with Bob barking happily and running around her in excited circles.

Hooks the butler opened the front door and welcomed them in. 'Your father is in the study, Miss,' he said, and she ran delightedly to see her father, who was sitting waiting by the roaring fire. He stood and gave her a big hug, and then Mrs. Hands brought in freshly baked pastries and tea. Bob sat at The Girl's feet while she warmed herself by the fire and told her daddy what had happened and how Bob

had kept her warm as toast.

'You're a good boy, Bob,' he said, stroking Bob's head

fondly. Bob looked at The Big Man's two huge Wolfhounds,

Brian and Boru, who lay sleeping in front of the fireplace,

and who both looked back as though to say, Well Done,

little man.

After sitting with daddy for some time, The Girl said that

she was going up to her room, and so Bob trotted upstairs

with her. She spent the rest of her day unpacking,

organising and tidying, and when she was finished she took

out her favourite book. It was growing cold so she and Bob

lay beneath the quilt and were very cosy as she read. Bob

was happy to be with his favourite person in the world, and

though he was not sure what books were, he listened

carefully when the girl began to read a passage to him. Bob was a very content little fellow. Being with The Girl was his Number One Job!

Bob was a very content little fellow.

Over the next week, the snow continued to fall, and it lay deeper and deeper so that the entire countryside became quiet and sleepy, covered in a white blanket. Bob spent a lot of time with The Girl in her room, sitting with her as she read her books, or as she wrapped the Christmas gifts she had made at school.

For Stan, she had knitted a long oatmeal-coloured woollen scarf, for Mrs. Hands she had made a mug in her pottery class: it featured the name Mrs. Hands written on the side, and though it was slightly wobbly in shape, she hoped Mrs. Hands would like it. For every member of the household there was a gift, and each gift was wrapped carefully in fresh brown paper, tied with a string and label. Bob couldn't say what The Girl was doing, a lot of things people did were strange to him, but he didn't mind because he was able to spend time with the girl, and she would talk to him as she worked, telling him about school and chatting about many things.

Bob watched her as she worked.

Bob listened carefully, and sometimes he would tilt his head to one side as he heard words he understood. After each present was wrapped and labelled, The Girl would place it carefully on her shelf, then sit back down at her little table and begin to wrap the next. Bob watched her as she worked, and he was very content.

Every afternoon The Girl wrapped herself up in hat, coat, scarf and wellington boots, a thick woollen pullover and her hiking corduroys, and she and Bob would go for a walk. One day they walked as far as the barrows, close to where earlier in the year, Bob had rescued The Girl from Angus the Bull. Bob growled at the memory. If Angus dared to return, Bob would see him off!

On other days they would walk around the house and then visit Stan in the Stables. 'Good afternoon, Miss,' Stan said one day, bending down to scratch Bob's ear. Stan went to a crate in the corner and took out two wizened apples, one each for the Big Man's two horses. 'An apple a day,' he said, 'Keeps the doctor away.'

Every day, the snow lay deeper and deeper.

'Those apples look very old,' Celia said, frowning at the old

fruit.

'I keep them dry in this box, see, and it doesn't matter if

they get a bit wrinkly, the horses still enjoy them.'

After speaking to Stan, Celia and Bob often went into the

walled garden. Being winter, everything was asleep and

quiet. Old Tom the gardener only came up to the Big House

once a week during the winter, to "see to his seedlings" and keep the place tidy, otherwise the garden was empty. Bob and the Girl went into the greenhouse and sat watching the snow falling.

Every day, the snow lay deeper and deeper. So deep in fact that, later that week, Stan had to go and borrow Old Helen again and hitch up the sleigh, in order to go to the nearby village of Cornhill to buy provisions for the Christmas celebrations.

One morning, Bob sat watching as Hooks the Butler set up a fir tree in the living room, and then he decorated it with papers streamers and shiny ornaments. Hooks then carried coal and wood and old newspapers to the large fireplace, and lit the fire. As it began to burn, the ornaments glittered and glowed, reflecting the flames. The coal fire, now lit, would be kept burning until the end of February.

Bob thought the room was perfect for lying comfortably and snoozing. He watched as The Girl helped out, placing candles around the room and hanging streamers from the door and the windows. Meanwhile Grace, the maid, who'd been collected by Stan in the old sleigh, was dusting and decorating the hall. Even the Big Man's study was hung with tinsel and decorations, though his two wolfhounds, Brian and Boru would not sit still for The Girl to wrap their collars in tinsel.

In the kitchen, Mrs. Hands decorated the Christmas cake and prepared Christmas puddings using the fruit she had carefully preserved since the summer. Bob was especially keen on the kitchen at this time, as there were a lot of spare ingredients, though Mrs. Hands knew not to give him raisins or chocolate, which were not good for a little brown dog (even though that same little brown dog would have eaten them up if he'd had the chance).

As preparations were made for Christmas, the snow continued to fall, blotting out lanes and paths, blocking roads, and turning the entire region into a quiet world in which very little moved. The wiser creatures slept deep in their burrows, and only a few hardy birds sang as they sat on bare branches or on top of old fence posts.

Everyone was busy decorating, cooking, fetching people, collecting provisions and wrapping presents. Bob had a lot of things to keep an eye on, because looking after the people in the Big House was his Number One Job, so every day he would go from room to room, watching people as they worked. Then, in the afternoons, he would go back to his kennel and keep an eye on the drive to watch for visitors.

Christmas Eve

The gifts were wrapped. The food was prepared. Mrs.

Hands had set her alarm clock for very early in the

morning in order to cook the goose. The pudding had been

made over a month earlier, when Mrs. Hands had asked

Grace to give the mix a final stir and make a wish. Grace

did just that, though she told no one the secret of what

she wished for.

The Big Man allowed Bob to sit in The Girl's room until well

after bed-time. Then finally, he came upstairs, knocked

and entered, wished Celia goodnight, told her that Father

Christmas would not visit until she was sound asleep (and

he would know if she was pretending), then gave her a big

daddy-hug. He clicked his tongue, 'Come along Bob,' he said.

After getting one final cuddle from The Girl, Bob turned

and followed the Big Man downstairs and through the house. The Big Man opened the door and let Bob out. Now, it might seem cruel to put a dog in a kennel on a long winter's night, especially when the snow lies deep. But border terriers have a double coat designed especially for the winter, and Bob's kennel was very cosy. It had a big old woollen blanket inside, that had been donated by The Girl when Bob was still a puppy, and even now it still had her special scent. Stan had tacked an old curtain to the top of the kennel door so that when Bob went into his kennel, it swung over the entrance and kept out the wind. Between the blanket, the curtain and his own warm coat, Bob was lovely and snug in his little home.

Nevertheless, Bob was a curious little fellow and he lay with his nose poking out of the doorway, keeping watch on the Big House and watching the snow fall from the sky. He knew that keeping the people in the house safe was his

Number One Job!

Bob's kennel was very cosy.

Bob's extra powerful hearing told him that Hooks the

Butler was walking round the house, switching off the

lamps, and dowsing the candles. Then he heard Hook's

bedroom door close. There was silence for a while until,

finally, Bob heard the Big Man leave his office and walk

upstairs to his own room. Bob felt content. His family were

asleep and, just in case anything occurred, Bob was on the spot ready to deal with it. He yawned, then stretched, then turned and went back inside his kennel, walked around in a tight circle as all dogs do before they lie down, then he settled, yawned again, closed his eyes and fell into a deep doggy sleep, where he dreamed of chasing Mr. Fox across wintry fields. Outside the kennel, the wind howled, the snow fell deeper and deeper, and if you had looked at the landscape from above, you would not have been able to tell field from road or hill from dale. The entire countryside was one large blanket of white. There were occasional homes and farms, from whose chimney's smoke rose and curled, but otherwise, the land slept, invisible and quiet beneath the snow. Bob slept quietly too, occasionally whimpering or giving little barks as he dreamed of rescuing

The Girl from giant foxes that he saw off with lots of barks and bites!

Sometime in the very middle of the night, Bob woke to a strange noise. In the far distance he could hear the faint sound of animals panting and bells jingling. And a human voice shouting in a loud cheerful voice. Very odd, he thought. Alert now, he peeped out from behind the curtain that hung at the front of his kennel. He made a noise that sounded like a question mark. *Mmmhh?* then he looked up at the clear sky from which stars twinkled down. He knew that each star was one of his ancestors, looking down on him and on the world, keeping an eye on things.

The strange noise grew louder until suddenly, from out of the sky, wooshed a sleigh. It was like the one that Stan had been using, but much larger and grander, bright-painted, with the wooden panels carved in intricate patterns, and unlike Stan's sleigh, which was pulled by Old Helen, this sleigh was pulled by eight deer, of a type Bob had never seen before. 'Whoaaa!' a voice shouted and the sleigh skidded to a halt in front of the Big House.

 In the sleigh sat a large, jolly-faced man with a long white beard. He was wearing a thick green fur-trimmed coat with a hood, also fur-trimmed, and heavy leather gloves. Behind the man was a huge sack, and the sack was full of parcels and packages, each with a label. Bob remembered labels from his adventure with Wee Jock the postman. This was very strange, so Bob decided he had better go investigate. He trotted over to the sleigh, sniffed warily at the large animals at the front and then went to the side and looked up at the man. 'Ho ho, little fellow! Do you live here?' the man asked in a large booming voice.

Bob gave a little bark. Usually he did not understand all the words that people said but in this case he understood perfectly, and the big bearded man seemed to understand Bob too. 'You do? Well that's very good news. Do you know this area well?'

Bob barked twice this time. He knew the local area very well. The man unfolded a very old map. 'Just as well, because, for the first time in more years than I care to admit, I'm bloomin' lost! This map was made during the time of James the Sixth,' he leaned over to Bob and whispered 'He was on the *naughty* list, you know!' Then he turned the map one way, then another, frowning. 'So it's a little bit out of date.' He looked down at Bob keenly. 'If I tell you the names of the families, do you think you could point me in the direction of their homes?'

Bob barked again, very happy that he could be helpful to

this strange man and his flying sleigh, pulled by eight large

deer.

**In the sleigh sat a large, jolly-faced man
with a long white beard.**

'Well, let's not waste time. Hop in!' said the man, opening a

door. Bob jumped in and scrabbled onto the seat beside

the man. Despite the cold, it was very cosy here, especially

when the man wrapped his heavy coat around Bob's

shoulders and patted his head. 'Well, Bob,' the man said

(how did he know Bob's name?), 'My name is Niklaus, and I

have some deliveries to make. Can you tell me where the

Bryson family live?'

Bob barked and looked over his shoulder.

'That way, eh?' And the man picked up the reins, gave them

a flick and shouted, 'Dancer, Prancer, away!' and the sleigh

moved forward as the reindeer began to run, then it lifted

smoothly into the air and began to fly! Bob looked down at

the ground as it disappeared, giving a short yelp of

concern. 'Don't you worry, little man, we're quite safe,' the

jolly man said, so Bob stared in the direction of the Bryson

cottage and no more than a minute later the sleigh touched

down again and the man, who was a lot lighter on his feet

than he appeared, took two presents from his sack, jumped from the sleigh, and somehow, magically, leapt right up onto the roof of the cottage, where he disappeared down the chimney!

At this, Bob gave another little yelp of alarm, and one of the deer turned around to him and said, 'Don't you worry about Niklaus, little one. He's been doing it a long time.'

Bob looked at the deer and said, 'Who are you?'

'I'm Blixen,' she told him. Then she introduced all the other deer, who said hello in turn.

'Who is that man?' Bob asked.

'That is Father Christmas,' Blixen told him. 'He brings gifts to every house in the world on Christmas Eve.'

'But why does he do that?' Bob asked Blixen. 'It seems very strange.'

'He's been doing it for so long, I couldn't tell you why,

except that he is kind and jolly and he brings joy to the

world.'

Suddenly, Father Christmas returned. 'Sorry for the delay,

they left a slice of cake. And a glass of sherry.' He burped

loudly then closed the door of the sleigh, picked up the

map and turned to Bob. What about the Wynd household?'

Bob knew these people too. On his regular jaunts with

Stan, or with Hooks when he went into the village for

supplies, Bob had visited all of the houses in the area. He

twisted in his seat and gave a bark. 'South-west. Right!'

Father Christmas picked up the reins and gave a cry,

'Away!'

And so it went on, Bob using his nose to smell the right

direction and point the way to each home, whereupon

Father Christmas would land, disappear onto the roof with

a handful of gifts, then return, often having eaten a slice

of cake or drinking a glass of milk or sherry. His coat

seemed to get tighter and his round tummy got larger

after each visit. They visited Farmer Douglas' house and

dropped off a gift for him and for Mrs. Douglas. They

visited the tiny cottage where Grace the kitchen maid

lived with her parents and all of her brothers and sisters.

Father Christmas delivered a large handful of gifts.

'Mustn't forget this,' he said, returning to grab a small

package, 'There's been a new delivery in the Merton

household.'

In this manner, they visited every home in the area.

'Hmm...' Father Christmas said at one point. He turned to

Bob. 'Do you know where the Cotton farm is?' and Bob gave

a cheerful yelp and off they set. After gifts had been

delivered to the Cottons, instead of flying away, the

reindeer pulled the sleigh a few hundred yards across a snow-covered field to an old barn, from where cosy lamplight glowed. From his sack of gifts, Father Christmas took a large bottle, wrapped in brown paper with a label, then leapt off the sleigh and strode towards the barn. Bob jumped down and followed him into the barn where he saw an old caravan and an untethered horse, who stood munching food from a bag. 'It's you then?' said an old man's quavery voice, and Bob barked happily. It was John Tinkle – Tinks! - the traveling musician and knife-grinder who had once rescued Bob after he got lost. Tinks was sitting on a stool and there was an empty seat beside him, two plates and two glasses, almost as though he expected a guest to arrive at any moment. 'Merry Christmas John Tinkle!' Niklaus said in his loud, hearty voice.

'And te yasel, Niklaus.' He turned to Bob, 'I see you've

brought ma wee pal wi' ye,' and he stroked Bob's head. 'Set

yourself down for a minute,' Tinks said. 'I have a wee cake.

We can wash it down with a dram.'

'I have a wee cake. We can wash it down with a dram.'

He unwrapped the bottle and without further talk he

poured them both a large glass. 'Merry Christmas John

Tinkle!' Father Christmas, said, and they clinked glasses

merrily.

Father Christmas sat on a stool beside John Tinkle and explained the situation with the snow and the map, so Bob trotted up the steps of the caravan to see Hamish the very old Scots Terrier who lived there. Hamish was asleep, and Bob saw his mush was even more grey than the last time. He nuzzled Hamish affectionately but didn't wake him, then he looked out of the caravan window and saw that Tinks and Father Christmas were deep in conversation. He lay down beside Hamish and fell asleep. Map reading was a tiring business!

Bob woke to find himself being carried very gently back to the sleigh. The Jolly Old Man sat Bob down at his side and then, with a cry to the Reindeer, they flew off into the night sky. Every time Bob was given a name he either pointed his nose, or barked in a certain direction, and off they flew to deliver gifts. Bob was very proud that he was able to help Father Christmas find his way around the

borders.

'One more stop for you, Bob,' the jolly old man shouted

above the noise of the wind, and suddenly the sleigh landed

again on the drive at the Big House. Father Christmas

picked up a number of gifts and left the sleigh, leaping

magically right up onto the high roof and disappearing into

the darkness.

Presently, he returned. 'You have been a great help to me,

tonight, Bob,' he told the little brown dog, and stroked his

fur fondly, his eyes sparkling and kindly, 'But now I must go

to Carlisle, where the roads are clearer, and I must leave

you behind to look after your family.'

Bob gave a bark, and jumped out of the sleigh and into the

soft snow, because looking after his family was his Number

One Job. He stood on his hind legs while he was petted

again, and he licked Father Christmas' mush too, which was even greyer than Old Hamish who lived in the caravan with John Tinkle.

He stood back down onto all four legs and watched as Father Christmas got back in his sleigh. 'Goodbye, Bob,' said Blixen, then he was wished goodbye by all the other reindeers too. Father Christmas, reins in hand, leaned over the side of the sleigh and ruffled Bob's head. 'You are a very helpful boy, Bob. I wish you a long and happy life.' And with that, he flicked the reins, and shouted 'Away!' The sleigh rose magically into the sky and flew across the moon, leaving behind a little brown dog who stared at the sky for a long while. Then he trotted happily back to his kennel. Bob had been helpful and he felt very proud.

**The sleigh rose magically into the sky
and flew across the moon.**

Bob shook the snow from his fur and then pushed past the

heavy sheet and entered his cosy little kennel. He was very

tired after his adventure with the jolly old man, so he

curled up on the girl's blanket and fell into a deep. happy

sleep. Outside, the sky turned grey again as snow began to fall onto the Big House, and onto the small cosy kennel, but inside, all was toasty and well.

Christmas morning.

The sky was clear and the fields surrounding the big house were white and crisp. The fence-posts were capped with snow, the lanes covered, the trees glazed in ice and snow. Even the river was iced along the edges, with only a clear lane in the middle where the icy water ran and burbled free. Bob slept late, his adventures of the previous night had made him tired, and so he missed the first hubbub of people rising and wishing each other Merry Christmas, sharing hugs and handshakes and greetings of Comfort and Joy.

Around seven in the morning, while the December sky was still dark, Stan hitched the sleigh to Old Helen, who Farmer Douglas had kindly loaned for the duration - he had another large horse, Goldie, who was Helen's foal from seven years ago and was even bigger and stronger. So, horse and sled journeyed out from the Big House to pick up the various members of the household who would be coming to back for a Christmas breakfast. For, every year, on Christmas Day, Mrs. Hands allowed The Big Man to use her kitchen and he prepared breakfast for his household, cooking an enormous meal for the people who worked in his home, wishing them Merry Christmas and giving out gifts.

And so it was that around nine in the morning, Stan returned with a sleigh full of people: Grace the maid had brought her youngest-but-one sibling, Charlie. Mrs. Hands brought her old dad, Gaffer Noble who'd been a farm hand, before retiring to a cottage in the village of Duddo, at the sprightly age of seventy-five. Old Tom the gardener was collected too, and Farmer Douglas, who marvelled at how well Stan managed Old Helen, along with Mrs. Douglas who had brought two of her famous seed cakes as a gift to the house.

At the front door of the Big House, they all dismounted and the Big Man welcomed them inside. Bob was awake by now and he ran around to the front door barking and leaping up at and licking at the guests in his friendly way. They all walked into the main dining room where places had been set, and Bob watched as the Big Man and the Girl served a huge, cooked breakfast, followed by tea and cakes, and large drams for Farmer Douglas, Tom the Gardener, and Gaffer Noble The Big Man then gave out gifts and thanked everyone for their hard work this year, and then sat down to eat with them and chat, and everyone wished each other Merry Christmas and exchanged gifts. The Girl turned on the radio and they all listened to the music that was played by the BBC.

Bob watched with pride as the Girl was allowed to open her presents too. From her daddy she received a scarf, a doll, and three brand new books. From Stan she received a lovely soft toy Border Terrier that looked just like Bob, and from Mrs. Hands a knitted woollen hat and mittens. In fact, she received lots of nice gifts. In return she gave Stan the scarf she had knitted him, and Mrs. Hands got her wobbly mug, and everyone gave and received gifts and were as happy for the giving as the receiving.

Finally, all the presents had been presented, except for one. The Girl said, 'And here's a present for Bobby.' She put it on the floor beside Bob and he could smell there was something nice inside, and he licked and sniffed at the paper, but in the end The Girl had to open it for him. It was a lovely new blanket she had crocheted for him while she was at school, that he could have an extra blanket in his kennel for those especially cold winter nights. Bob was

delighted because it had The Girl's smell on it and he loved

her the best. He barked and then skedaddled around the

room with the corner of the blanket in his teeth, dragging

it along behind him. Everyone laughed at his antics. Then

Mrs. Hands, saw something still hanging on the tree and

said, 'What is that?' so the Big Man stood, went to the

tree and picked up a small gift that was hanging there. He

unwrapped it and inside was a brand-new collar for Bob,

engraved with his name and address:

Bob
The Kennel
Craigmorley House
The Borders

And there was a note attached, written in fine calligraphy:

To Bob and on the other side it said, *For being such a good boy.* The Big Man said, 'It has no name attached. I wonder who it's from?'

Bob knew who it was from. He remembered his journey the night before with the kindly old man in his magical sleigh, pulled by eight reindeer. He remembered the kind words of Blixen, and sitting in the cosy barn with Father Christmas and Tinks the Traveller, and seeing Toby the horse and old sleepy Hamish. This collar came in very handy a long time later, as we'll find out in a different story.

'This is for you, Bob,' the Big Man said, bending down and fastening on his collar.

'He's a braw wee doggie,' said old Douglas, who kept collies, and judged dogs purely on their ability to help out the running of a farm, 'I've no doubt he keeps away the vermin and foxes.'

Bob was very pleased with all the attention he was getting. By the end of the breakfast, he had eaten more scraps than he could remember, and he had gotten lots of pets and kind words.

"To Bob. For being such a good boy."

Afterwards, Stan returned the guests to their homes in the sleigh, while the Girl and the Big Man got ready for church. Bob wasn't allowed to go to church, so he stayed back with Grace, the kitchen maid, who followed the old religion, and had gone to church at midnight, and he was allowed to sit in the kitchen and watch as she prepared

Christmas dinner.

'You stay here, Bob, and look after the house,' The Girl had

told him, before she left for church. Bob did his best to

look after the house as he was instructed, though for most

of the morning he simply sat and watched as Grace

prepared the food. Every now and again, Grace would give

Bob another treat.

He was very proud of doing his job.

And so Christmas continued, with everyone giving each

other good wishes and cheer, whether it was with kind

words or a wee dram, or in Bob's case, by giving him lots of

attention and strokes.

*

Over the next few days, Bob spent a lot of time with The

Girl, walking snow-drifted lanes, and through fields. Robin

Redbreasts sang their songs perched on old gateposts, and the river grew so frozen it was almost possible to walk from one side to the other – only the narrowest part of the middle kept flowing. Once or twice on his morning rounds Bob spotted Mr. Fox's pawprints or smelled his scent, but he never caught him, nor did Mr. Fox manage to raid the chicken coop, so all was well.

One day, just before New Year's Eve, Bob was even allowed to accompany the Big Man on a walk with his two wolfhounds. The Big Man was visiting some old friends, and he took along a bottle of the good stuff. Bob felt very proud to be included in this walk, but usually he spent this time between Christmas and New Year with The Girl. Because being with The Girl was his Number One Job!

New Year's Eve

Just across the border, at the end of a long and lonely lane, is a picture-book cottage owned by a little old lady called Mrs. Darling, and her pet bulldog, Edward. Despite the cottage being "out of the way", for many years, indeed, for decades, this little old lady has held a Hogmanay celebration for her friends and the locals who live within a few miles of her home.

Hogmanay is the Scottish word for New Year's Eve, and every year this little old lady put out food and drink, and played gramophone music and her visitors would stay until well after midnight, to see in the New Year and wish each other well.

Edward, her bulldog, being of the breed known as the King of Dogs, liked to spend some time in the little old lady's home with the throng, bestowing his goodwill and eating

pieces of pie, but when old Gregor MacGregor took out his

bagpipes for all the guests to dance to, Edward knew it was

time to retire to his kennel. His sensitive ears did not like

the skirl of the pipes, he thought it sounded like a

thousand cats singing badly. Plus, one of the dancers might

chance to step on his paws! He left the picture-book

cottage and padded through the snow to his kennel where

he curled up and lay down with a full tummy, content while

the party continued.

After some hours the last of the guests went home with a

wish and a cheer, and the cottage became quiet. The old

lady cleaned away the remnants of the party and then she

came out into the garden to check on Edward and tuck him

into his kennel. After she had gone, he lay snug, his tummy

full of treats and his sleepy imagination beset with scenes

of himself seeing off bulls with a growl, or a nip from his

powerful jaws. Outside, the wind and snow picked up as a

winter's storm began to rage in the night sky.

At the end of a long and lonely lane
is a picture book cottage.

Edward's breed are known for their ability to "service a

bull" – that is, to chase off an errant bull if one decides to attack. Edward had never had to fight a bull, but he lived

in hope. Amidst his dreams, on this Hogmanay night

however, Edward's rest was disturbed by a strange noise.

'Pssst!'

Edward opened a sleepy eye.

'Pssst!'

'Who is outside of my door?' Edward asked in his rumbly

voice.

'It's me. Pssst! It's Reynard. Can I come in? It's blinkin'

freezing out here!' and at that moment a sharp red nose

poked through the entrance to Edward's kennel.

Edward was somewhat taken aback at the entrance of

Reynard, Mr. Fox himself, but he reminded himself that

the King of Dogs should always share his shelter with

lesser creatures and so he said, 'Come in, Mr. Reynard.'

Then he moved to one side to make space for the fox.

'Would you like to sleep here tonight?' asked Edward. 'I

don't mind sharing, and it's very cosy.'

**The two animals, Bulldog and Fox, snuggled
close together inside Edward's kennel.**

'Would I ever!' said Reynard, who snuggled in beside him.

'It's too shivery out there, and snow has blocked up my

den.'

'Then you're very welcome to stay,' Edward said kindly.

'Some dogs don't like foxes,' Reynard said, suspiciously.

'I am a bulldog. I only take against bulls, and even then, only when they behave in a rambunctious manner.'

'Well, that's fortunate,' Reynard said, 'Because I'm not a bull.'

'Indeed,' said Edward.

And so it was that the two animals, Bulldog and Fox, snuggled closer together inside Edward's kennel. They were an unlikely pair, but their combined heat made the kennel very snug, while outside, a snowstorm began to rage, and the other creatures of this winter world slept quietly and deep. As he slept, Edward dreamt of valiantly chasing bulls away from little old ladies in distress while Reynard, asleep beside him, dreamt of chasing chickens around their coop. And just a few miles away on the other side of the border, in a different kennel, at the side of the Big House, a little brown dog lay on the blanket crocheted by his Girl, resplendent in his fresh new collar, and he dreamt happily

of chasing Reynard.

***

And on that cosy note, dear reader, we'll leave Border Bob,

Edward the King of Dogs, and naughty Mr. Reynard to their

sleep, not forgetting the Girl, Mrs. Hands, Stan the

Stableboy and all the other characters we've met in this

little storybook, set on the borders of England and

Scotland, during the Season of Goodwill.

For lovers of dogs big and small, of every colour, breed and

variety, but especially for those who share their lives with

little brown dogs...

Merry Christmas
and a Happy New Year!

...Bob

The **Border Bob** series:

- The Adventures of Border Bob.

- Border Bob's Christmas

- The Friends of Border Bob will be released in

  time for Christmas 2024.

For enquiries contact www.jamesross.media.

Printed in Great Britain
by Amazon

11873596R00047